# UNLABELED

# UNLABELED

By
Trudy Harvey Tait

Harvey Christian Publishers Inc.
449 Hackett Pike, Richmond, KY 40475
Email: books@harveycp.com
www.harveycp.com
Tel. 423 768 2297

ISBN 978-1-932774-86-3
Printed in USA

Cover Design by
Vladyslav Vitel
VladyslavVitel@gmail.com

Printed by
Lightning Source
La Vergne, TN 37086

# CONTENTS

# Prologue
# It happened in Africa

Rahela Morgan tiptoed along the tiled hallway, holding her breath. A hyena howled in the distance. Her dog, Titan, barked in reply. But in the house, no one stirred, not even her old nurse, Deborah, who had ears like a hawk and a nose for sniffing out trouble.

"So far, so good," thought Rahela, as she slipped into the bathroom and closed the door softly behind her. She fumbled in the pocket of her pajamas for the precious packet she had bought that day at the pharmacy in Mombasa, fifty miles away. Morning sickness for several weeks had made her determined to know the worst.

A few moments later, it was all done. There, in front of her, lay the evidence, just as she had thought. "Precious new life," her mother had told her when she had become pregnant with Rahela's younger sister who had died of cerebral malaria at age six.

Rahela grabbed the edge of the sink for support. Was her mother rejoicing with God at that very moment over this "precious new life" that was growing within her daughter's belly, or was she weeping? No, there are no tears in Heaven, Rahela told herself. Anyway, her mother was dead, and God was an eternity away.

She could tell her Dad, or rather, she *should* tell her Dad. Poor Dad! He'd take it very hard. He blamed himself for what had happened that dreadful night, two months before.

"I was a sucker, Rahela," he had confessed more than once. "Your mother always said I was too gullible. She was right." Then he would sit, head in hands, for a long time.

It had all been so very evil and so well planned! He had received news that one of his best workers had had an accident on the tractor. Only he hadn't. It was all a ruse. And then the generator failing! The devil couldn't have planned it better. Well, the perpetrator was a devil, as far as Rahela was concerned, or as near one as a human could be. She had never liked him even as a child when he had worked on their plantation and had been relieved when he had been sent to jail in faraway Mombasa for thieving. Only no one on their plantation had realized that the villain had been released on bail and was free to do his worst.

Rahela's eyes fell on the telltale test strip. Her father's answer to the police when they had come to question everyone came back to her with sickening force.

"Do you report anything stolen, Mr. Morgan?" the senior officer had asked as a matter of routine. "Yes," Marvin had answered heavily. "Something that can never ever be either truly evaluated or reimbursed—my daughter's virginity. That's what was stolen."

Those words had shocked the police, but it had only been a partial answer. Ask any rape victim and they'll tell you that. Just all she had lost, Rahela supposed she'd be discovering until the day she died.

The clock in the hallway struck two. She had to get to her room before Deborah discovered her. Not that she could hide anything for long from this faithful, loving woman who had served her family for as long as Rahela could remember. She knew she'd eventually have to tell her everything, though before or after she "did it" she wasn't sure. She could imagine the advice Deborah would give: "Child, a life is a life. Whatever has happened, it's your baby. God can make something beautiful come from all this. But whatever you do, you've got to let it live."

"Let it live!" Rahela stuffed the edge of her pillow into her mouth. She felt like screaming. That's exactly what she could never do. She hated that thing inside her—she wouldn't even call it "him" or "her" though of course it had to be a boy or girl. Wouldn't it be a greater sin to grow a monster and let it loose into the world, than to snuff it out when it was barely existing? She'd go back to the city tomorrow; she'd find a doctor who understood—not the missionary doctor who had tended her mother during her illness, but some quack, it didn't matter who. No one need know about this "act" she was about to do, though everyone for miles around had already heard about the rape. Bush telegraph may be an ancient mode of communication but it is a highly effective one.

"Poor Miss Rahela!" they were all saying. "Why did it have to happen to our little missy?" The sympathy, of course, all lay with her. But if it was ever discovered what she was about to do, that would all change. "Murderer," they'd call her. She shuddered. Did she want that word branded on her for life?

A hyena howled again, this time much nearer. As usual, Titan barked in reply. Rahela lay down flat on her bed. Her two hands began slowly to feel around her abdomen. Gradually they formed fists and soon she was pummeling her stomach for all she was worth. She began moaning softly in rhythm. Then louder and louder her voice rose.

"Rahela, child, what on earth are you doing?"

Rahela stopped moaning, stopped pummeling, and sat bolt upright. Wild-eyed, she stared into her nurse's familiar face.

"It's just me, Miss Rahela. Just me."

Rahela felt Deborah's ample arms engulf both her and the "thing" she was carrying inside her.

"Is it them nightmares again?" Deborah asked.

Rahela shook her head. "It's worse than that Deborah. Much worse."

"Then what, on God's good earth, can it be? You were going crazy, Miss Rahela."

Rahela knew what would happen if she told her nurse the whole truth. She wouldn't have the guts to act for herself. Someday soon she would have to tell her, but not now. Her lips set in a straight line and then she said defiantly, "I'm not telling you! So that's that!"

Deborah gave one of her "stupendous sighs" as Rahela called them. Then the light began to dawn. What would cause her dear, precious girl to nearly lose her senses? Only one thing, one awful, terrible thing!

"Oh, dear God!" Deborah gasped, flopping to her knees and burying her head in the blankets. "You're pregnant!"

# Chapter One
# Playing the detective
## 1.

"This suitcase has no label, Susan," I announced to the girl sitting behind the large, metal desk in the left-luggage office at Swansea airport. I was dog tired. It had been a very long day. I sighed impatiently as I lugged the heavy, bright red suitcase across the floor and stood it upright in the corner of the room. This job often bored me to tears and, right now, I was not a bit interested in dealing with lost luggage. But I had no choice. Holiday jobs were scarce and I needed the money. Students at Swansea Bible College were notoriously short on cash and I was no exception.

Susan glanced at the suitcase and frowned. She frowned pretty often. Can't say I blamed her exactly. Her job was pretty frustrating at times. "I hate untagged luggage," she fumed. She was obviously as tired as I was. "Why can't people be reasonable? Bags without a label mean a lot more work for all of us."

I nodded sympathetically. "Sure do, but the tags can fall off, you know."

Susan shrugged. "Then folks should fasten them on better," she countered. "Labels are so important—tell you a lot about the person."

"A lot about a person?" I repeated, half to myself.

"Yes, where they're going, of course; and where they come from, and...." She hesitated.

"And what else?" I wanted to know.

"Well," she began, and then stopped short as her eyes fell on something white and shiny lying by the office door.

I followed her gaze. "It's the lost label!" I exclaimed, stooping to pick it up. "Miss Rahela Morgan, Rosedale Christian College, Moreton, NC." I read the words aloud as I handed Susan the luggage tag.

She stared at it for a long time. "Sounds familiar," she mused. "I think Miss Rahela Morgan has already reported her lost luggage."

"Oh yes?" I said with a grin. "And I bet she was short and slightly plump with long dark hair, and spoke with a bit of a foreign accent, right?" I don't know why I said this except, as I said before, I was bored to tears, and playing the guessing game seemed the thing to do right then.

Susan placed the label in front of her and looked up at me, a new respect dawning in her eyes. Then she grinned. She was actually rather pretty when she smiled, which wasn't often. "How on earth did you guess?" she muttered.

"Easy," I told her loftily. "Labels tell you a lot about a person, don't they? Isn't that what you've just said?"

"I know, but..."

"But what? Rahela—sounds Spanish, doesn't it? And Morgan—well that's certainly a Welsh surname. You should know that. And the suitcase has come from Nairobi via Heathrow, so she's most likely a missionary's kid going to some Christian college or other in the States. And, if she's lived abroad for years, she probably has a bit of an accent."

Susan's grin grew wider. "Detective Potter, pleased to meet you," she said, holding out her hand."

I shook it formally. "My pleasure, Miss Martin. Leave the case to me. I'll get to the bottom of it in no time."

My attempt at a pun made her groan. "You've been reading too many detective stories, Mark," Susan told me. "But Sherlock would be proud of you. This Morgan girl *was* small and plumpish, with long dark hair and she did have a rather peculiar accent. But Spanish—Welsh—I'm not certain about that."

"But you are sure the label belongs to her suitcase?" I wanted to know. It was nearly 9 pm and I knew we'd better settle this mystery before we both finished for the day.

"Pretty sure," Susan said, her usual, serious, over-efficient self once more. "She described it to me. I've got her paperwork right here on this desk. The suitcase is to be delivered, to, let's see; does the label give a Welsh address?" She turned the tag over as she spoke.

"Yes, it does," she said, sounding relieved. "A Swansea address, the same one the girl gave me this afternoon. She said she was visiting her Welsh grandmother over Christmas and then going on to the States. Actually, you're scheduled to deliver it tomorrow morning."

"You don't say!" I exclaimed, grinning. Susan had been reluctant, at first, to turn me loose in Swansea traffic. "You need more experience driving in the UK," she would tell me at least once a day. So this was going to be my first delivery.

"Remember you're in Great Britain, Mark," Susan warned as she gathered up her papers. "Think 'left, left, left.' And don't be asking our clients too many questions. You Yanks can be a bit over pushy at times. And this Rahela Morgan is our client, you know. Treat her with respect."

"As if I'd do anything else," I muttered. "I'll just be my charming self, Susan," I retorted. "Can't you trust me?"

"Oh, always, Mark, always," she assured me, and I really think she meant it.

## 2.

Miss Rahela Morgan had her suitcase delivered by noon the next day, which happened to be December 22, 1987. I'll always remember that day! It dawned dark and drizzly, just like a host of other days I'd passed in Wales over the past three months. I loved the UK but hated the weather. I'd been to England once before but had never visited Wales. Now I was living there for two whole years and would return home with a Bible School diploma tucked under my arm, all ready to face whatever life dished up to me, or so I hoped.

I shivered as I opened the truck door and stepped out onto the damp pavement. A few moments later, I was wheeling Rahela Morgan's large, bright red suitcase up the short path that led to the row of terraced houses which lined both sides of Hart Street. I stopped abruptly at No. 21.

The door opened almost before I had rung the bell. "Here's your luggage, Miss," I said respectfully, remembering Susan's advice. I said, "Miss," because I knew it was Rahela the moment I set my eyes on her—short, on the plump side, with long dark hair!

"Thanks. You've been very prompt," she told me politely. I smiled to myself. Another one up for me. This girl certainly *did* have a foreign accent, exactly as I had predicted.

"The label had come off," I found myself saying. "But we found it lying on the floor so…"

"Sorry about that," the girl said, reaching for the case. "I got Deborah to tie it on for me, but her fingers are crippled with arthritis. I ought to have done it myself."

I stole a fleeting glance at her face and made a mental note. "Attractive, smart, but probably spoilt rotten—waited on by a host of Deborahs all her life. And as naïve as they come. Doesn't look quite ready to make it on her own." Then I caught myself. I'd been trying to imagine who this Miss Rahela really was ever since I read that shiny label the night before, though why, I just couldn't say. Curiosity killed the cat, didn't it? I'd have to stop before it got me into a heap of trouble.

The girl reached for the suitcase. "It's very heavy," I warned. "Can I lift it in for you?"

Rahela nodded as I stepped into the hallway. "You're from the States, aren't you?" she asked, with just the hint of a smile.

"However did you guess?" I asked grinning. Now someone was turning the tables on me. "Playing detective?" I asked. It was out before I could help it.

"It doesn't take a detective to know where *you* come from!" she retorted.

I rather resented that, but of course she was right—short cropped hair, six foot two inches tall, broad-shouldered, brash, anything else? Oh yes. A good southern accent which I couldn't camouflage if I tried.

"And you," I retorted, feeling she was asking for all she could get. "You are half Spanish, half Welsh, probably spent your life in East Africa. And you're going to college in North Carolina." I paused to take a breath.

"Anything else?" The girl was baiting me now.

"Yes," I told her confidently. "You're probably a missionary's kid, away from home for the first time."

I was glad Susan couldn't see the look Miss Morgan gave me right then. "I'm sorry," I muttered, as I relinquished the handle of the suitcase and turned to go.

The girl's face relaxed. "It's OK," she reassured me. "I like Americans on the whole. They say what they think. Only you're wrong about one thing."

"I'm glad it's only one thing," I muttered, ready to make my escape.

"Actually, I should have said two things. Rahela isn't a Spanish name. It's Romanian for Rachel."

Now she had me! I'd made it pretty obvious I didn't know Spanish very well. "Yes," she went on, "my mother was Romanian; my father is Welsh." "*Was....is*," I noted to myself.

"And I'm not a missionary's kid," she informed me, "though I've met plenty, so they probably rubbed off on me." She glanced down at her pale blue sweater and denim skirt. "I…"

"Rahela, who are you talking to? Invite him in, won't you," a wheezy voice in a broad Welsh accent interrupted from an adjoining room. "The kettle's on the hob."

"OK, Grandma," Rahela called over her shoulder and then turned and smiled at me. Now, when Susan smiled, she was certainly pretty. But when this Welsh-Romanian girl smiled, a light bulb lit up inside of me that made me forget how damp and dismal it was outside.

"Yes, why don't you come in and have some tea?" Rahela suggested.

I followed the girl into the tiny living room where a white-haired little lady with eyes like Rahela's and skin amazingly smooth for her age, sat in her rocking-chair, covered by a plaid rug. A large, grey cat sat purring at her feet. The tea kettle whistled in the kitchen. A canary chirped from its cage by the window.

Half-an-hour passed before I knew it, and in that time, I had consumed two cups of tea poured from a truly English teapot and three of the most delicious scones I had ever tasted. Not only that, but Rahela and her grandmother had discovered almost all that was worth knowing about me. They knew that I had a twin sister; that my father was a pastor of an Independent Evangelical church in Eastern Tennessee; that I was attending Swansea Bible College because Dad was an avid admirer of its founder, Rees Howells, and that I wanted to be a vet eventually, if my well-meaning father didn't get his way and turn me into a preacher.

In return, I had learned, well, what had I learned? Only that Rahela's father owned a coffee plantation in Kenya; that her mother had died three years ago, and that she was going to eventually train to be a doctor and help children dying from the Aids epidemic in

East Africa. I suppose that was enough to know about anyone after a half-hour's chat, and yet, for me, it wasn't. It was far from enough. I desperately wanted to say, "Can I see you again?" But maybe it would be good to check her out a bit before I did that.

"You're going to a Christian college," I blurted out as I placed my empty teacup on the table and rose to go, "so that implies you're probably a Christian, right?"

If I'd asked her if she was a terrorist she couldn't have looked more shocked. Then I remembered that outside of the good old USA, you didn't go around asking strangers that question.

"Sorry," I muttered. "I shouldn't have asked that."

"It's OK," she said, but her voice sounded distant. "But maybe it's God you should be asking about that, not me."

I had no answer for that one. "Good-bye, Rahela," I muttered. I had reached the door by this time. "Thanks for the tea."

"You're very welcome. And thanks for delivering my suitcase."

"Safe travels to the US," I told her as I stepped onto the pavement.

"Thanks."

Our eyes met for only a second, but it was enough. I was not an experienced "soul-reader" but I knew instinctively that this girl had been wounded almost beyond repair. She certainly had not needed a blundering American to quiz her about her Christianity.

I leapt into my truck and zoomed down Hart Street. Then it hit me; I hadn't even told the girl my name, not that it mattered. I probably would never see her again which was just as well. Someone who couldn't answer a simple question might not be a person I wanted to get to know better.

"But she *did* answer you," a voice told me as I turned on to one of Swansea's busy main streets and headed east. "She told you to ask God, not her."

So, being the simple guy I am, I did just that. "God," I said, keeping my eyes wide open, of course, "is this girl a true Christian, someone I should get to know better or is she...?"

I stopped abruptly. What was I about to imply? That she might be an atheist or agnostic or maybe even worse?

"Oh, Rahela," I muttered as I neared the airport, "what have you done to me?"

"Well, Mark," Susan greeted me a few moments later. "Was this Rahela Morgan just like you expected?"

"Yes, and no," I muttered.

"Don't want to talk about her?" she went on. She was grinning now and I didn't like it.

"No, I don't. Why should I? She's just another client, isn't she?"

"Of course she is, Mark," Susan replied. Her grin had spread from ear to ear. "Of course she's just another client."

I turned and left the office in a black mood. Susan had upset me. Rahela had upset me. I'd stay away from all Welsh girls and Welsh-Romanian ones, too. American girls for American boys! That was definitely the safest route to take for a Southern guy like me.

# Chapter Two
## Second Impressions
### 1.

And so Rahela Morgan vanished from my life as quickly as she had entered it, or did she? Vanished is probably not the best word to use of someone who constantly invades your dreams.

"Who on earth is this Rahela?" my roommate once asked me. "You've talked about her at least twice in your sleep. "Is it your girlfriend back home? Only I thought her name was Amanda."

"Been snooping on me, have you?" I muttered, not sure whether to be annoyed or amused.

"Couldn't help noticing the name in the corner of those envelopes you receive every week," he explained.

"Amanda is *not* my girlfriend," I growled. "She's just a very old friend and next door neighbor. We grew up together."

"And this Rahela?" he wanted to know.

"She's a girl I met once, when I was working at Swansea airport," I told him.

"Just once?"

"Yes, just once."

My roommate stared at me, shook his head, shrugged his shoulders and muttered, "Must have been some girl!"

"She was," I muttered back.

"And she went in and out of your life, just like that?" he wanted to know.

"Yes, well, she came into it certainly. I don't think she's ever exited, though."

I know he thought me absolutely crazy. I thought so myself. So I made up my mind I'd ring Rosedale College when I got back home.

Whether I would have or not I never had the chance to discover. Providence, or fate if you like, took the decision completely out of my hands.

When I did finally return to the States one scorching afternoon in mid-June and stumbled up the verandah steps of our two-story, vinyl-sided farmhouse, Rahela Morgan was, for once, nowhere in my thoughts. After two long years abroad, all I wanted was to have Mom's arms around me, hear my twin sister's laughter and the welcoming bark of Captain, the huge, black, German shepherd who had guarded our house for at least eight years now. And I would even welcome Dad's lectures over breakfast. I'd sort of missed them all these months. All this I wanted very badly, but nothing more, at least not right then.

That was why I didn't know what I felt when, after all the bear-hugs, kisses, and tears, (women can't be happy without tears, at least the women in my life can't,) my twin sister whispered in my ear: "Hope you won't be mad at me, Mark, but I've agreed to let a foreign student spend the summer with us. I know you wrote that you were looking forward to being 'just family' again, but I couldn't resist. She seemed so lonely."

If the aroma of Mom's apple pies baking in the oven hadn't filled my nostrils right then, who knows what I might have whispered back to Kaye, but the prospect of one of my favorite deserts served with homemade ice cream made even the likelihood of a foreign girl invading our privacy all summer seem surprisingly bearable.

"It's OK," I whispered back. "I can't grumble at anything right now. Home feels and smells like Heaven."

That was when I saw *her*, sitting on a chair by the window, looking as if she were trying to make herself invisible—a small dark figure, on the plump side, with an abundance of long dark hair waving down to her waist. "The foreign girl," I noted to myself. Yet to me, at least, she didn't seem very foreign after all. In fact, she was strangely familiar.

The girl suddenly turned round. Her eyes stared confusedly into mine. I stared back in mute shock. Just then, Kaye came in between us and began introductions, but I didn't need them.

"Rahela!" I gasped, feeling my dreams were coming true, only it was all too sudden and too public!

## 2.

Overcome by jetlag I expected to fall asleep as soon as my head hit the pillow that first night home, but it wasn't like that. Meeting Rahela again had temporarily driven sleep away. I wasn't quite sure what to do with her. She was no longer some phantom princess who wove a spell over me while I slept. The girl of my dreams had taken on flesh and blood, and while it was, in many ways, truly delightful, it was also overwhelming. What was I supposed to do with this vision come to life? Welcome her as a long lost friend, which, of course, she wasn't? Treat her as a complete stranger, which she wasn't either? And another question: how had she landed in the hills of East Tennessee, of all places?

"My best friend, Janelle," Kaye explained over coffee the next morning, "goes to Rosedale and happens to be Rahela's roommate, so I met Rahela several times—at their school play, at a ball game, at MacDonald's. She couldn't go back to Kenya for the summer, so I invited her here." This explanation seemed to satisfy everyone but me. I was pretty sure that Kaye had met many foreign students in her three years at UNC and yet, as far as I knew, not one had been invited home.

"Know what I think, Mark?" my twin confided. "Rahela Morgan has been sent to us for a reason. I'm not quite sure what it is yet, but God's up to something, that's for sure."

"Isn't He always?" I retorted.

Kaye grinned. "Yes. Of course He is, but what? That's the tantalizing question. Maybe He thinks we all need shaking up a bit."

"We...what?" I gasped.

"Everything's so cut and dried in our family," Kaye explained. "Absolutely everything! And if anyone can do something about that, it'll be Rahela Morgan."

I held up my hand. "Slow down, Sis. It's my first morning home!"

"Sorry," she apologized. "I thought you already knew Rahela."

"Know her? Of course I don't know her. I only spoke to her for about half-an-hour eighteen months ago. That's not enough time to know anyone, is it?"

Kaye grinned. "Might be with some people, but not with Rahela. Then I suppose I know her the best of anyone in our family. We sometimes talk into the night."

"About what?" I wanted to know.

"Oh, Africa, America, college, and sometimes religion. She's fascinating. You can't label her."

"What do you mean?"

Kaye laughed tantalizingly. "Find out for yourself. Come with us tomorrow to the mountains?"

"Us?"

"Yes—me, Amanda, and Reg and...."

"Speaking of Amanda," I interrupted. "Where is she?"

"Dying to see you, of course," Kaye said. "She said she'd pop in this morning. She didn't want to interrupt our family reunion last night."

That didn't seem quite like Amanda. I thought she had considered herself a part of our family for as long as I could remember.

"Anything up?" I wanted to know.

"With Amanda?" Kaye asked. I nodded. "Nothing," she assured me, "except that she has grown up all of a sudden. And I think...." she broke off abruptly as the kitchen door opened behind me. I turned around and there stood the girl next door—the girl who had been my best friend for as long as I could remember—the girl who had written me faithfully every week for the past two years, and the girl who, I had been told repeatedly by my parents, would eventually make me the ideal wife.

I held out my arms. "It's so good to have you back," Amanda murmured in my ear.

"It's like heaven to be back," I whispered as I gave her a hug and then released her and took a step backwards.

"Amanda!" I gasped. The vision in front of me was totally other than the girl I remembered from two years ago.

Kaye laughed delightedly. "She's something else, isn't she!" she told me as she patted my arm.

"She's...." I began, but couldn't go on.

Amanda was blushing furiously by now. "I haven't changed inside, Mark," she stammered. "I've just grown up a bit, that's all."

That was an understatement! I had never imagined that my old playmate would evolve into this elegant beauty.

"You're not the only man who admires her," Kaye warned me. "So be prepared for some competition."

Amanda laughed lightly. I noted that her laugh, at least, hadn't changed at all. "He's not the only one who has rivals," she said softly, arching her eyebrows.

"That's probably true," Kaye agreed, giving me a wink. "This summer should prove very interesting!"

I stared from one girl to the other. Then the penny dropped. I opened my mouth to protest then closed it again promptly. I wouldn't argue. I'd simply prove them both wrong. I wasn't romantically interested in either Amanda or Rahela. The one was just a very old friend and the other a mere acquaintance. But as I went outside to help Dad with the haying, I knew I was kidding myself. I had been writing to the one girl every week for two years and had just been blown away by her beauty. And the other? I had merely dreamed about her night after night for weeks on end. That was all!

"Kaye's right as always," I muttered to myself as I hoisted a bale of hay onto the trailer. This summer should prove very interesting indeed!

### 3.

"You are coming with us to the mountains tomorrow, aren't you Mark?" I hated that my twin had to put me on the spot in front of everyone.

I had worked hard all day in the fields and was tucking into an enormous helping of homemade lasagna, one of my favorites. I had not seen Rahela since the previous evening, but now she was sitting opposite me, her large serious eyes fixed on my face.

"Not sure," I hedged. "Dad needs more help with the haying."

"Oh, come on," Kaye wheedled. "It is never the same without you. You'll manage quite well without him, won't you Dad?"

My father never could resist my twin sister so he nodded in acquiescence, his mouth full of lasagna. I knew, though, that he had been counting on my help to get the harvest in before the rain came.

"I'm going to stay and help you," I told him decisively. "We've only got a few more days of predicted good weather."

Kaye sighed resignedly while I thought I saw Rahela frown ever so slightly.

"Ok, then," my twin agreed. "I suppose we can put off our trip for a day or so, although it won't be the same if the weather breaks."

"Mark is going with you tomorrow," Dad announced, as he pushed his plate aside. "I'll get some neighbors in to help. I've managed two years without him so one more day won't make much difference."

I groaned inwardly. Back only one full day and now this! How would I cope with three girls, let alone Reg Perkins, Amanda's handsome and charming brother who had probably already swept the "foreign" girl off her feet! And yet, I reasoned, as I undressed that evening, maybe it wouldn't be so bad after all. Rahela and Reg, Amanda and myself. A foursome, with Kaye as chaperone. Perfect!

Somehow, though, it felt far from perfect when the five of us piled into Dad's station wagon the next morning.

"You drive, Mark," Kaye ordered. "And Rahela can sit up front with you. She'll see better that way."

I looked at the others. Reg was glaring at my sister, while Amanda refused to meet my eye.

"I've been driving on the left for two years," I reminded them. "I think it's best for one of you to drive."

"I'll do it," Reg volunteered cheerfully.

"No," Kaye countered. "It's my dad's car. My brother or I should drive. I'll do it if Mark won't."

So that's how it was—Kaye and Rahela up front, and the three of us in the back. I felt awkward at first, sitting next to my beautiful neighbor who seemed far more silent than the talkative teenager I remembered from two years back. But it wasn't long before old memories took precedent as we regaled each other with tales of past escapades.

"These two were inseparable," Reg informed Rahela as we stopped for gas.

"Obviously," Rahela commented, rather dryly, I thought.

"Yep!" Reg went on. "There was never anyone else in the picture, just them. And it seems nothing has changed!"

"I think a lot has changed," Kaye put in before I had a chance to comment. "They're not boy and girl anymore but sensible, grown adults. Now, Mark, I insist you drive. I'm tired and it's time you got into the swing of things again."

I shrugged and nodded. And as I got behind the wheel I decided it was best to go with the flow. Why not enjoy whatever or whoever Providence decided to put in my path and see where that led? And it was flattering to have such an avid listener. Appalachian history and folklore had always been my hobby and now it came in handy.

But my every watchful twin punctured my ego as usual when we stopped for lunch and had a moment alone together. "I know I made you drive, Mark," she whispered, but I didn't mean you to have eyes for no one but Rahela. Remember to be kind to Amanda."

"I always am," I whispered back.

"Maybe," she countered. "But it's obvious you have eyes for no one but Rahela. And that's fine with me, but please, make it a little less obvious. Amanda's hurt. Can't you see?"

Yes, I could see, and it bothered me. I really was fond of Amanda, so for the rest of the day, I obeyed my twin's instructions and was incredibly kind to my beautiful neighbor, insisting that Kaye drive home.

"You go to such extremes, Mark," Kaye scolded that evening after supper. "Now you're giving Amanda the wrong idea."

"Wrong idea?" I fumed. "I'm just obeying your orders."

Kaye put an arm around me. "Sorry," she said in her most contrite tone, "I know you tried but…."

I pushed her away. "Yes, I tried," I muttered. "And you manipulated me terribly, moving me like a pawn from front to back seat. I'm no good at paying attention to two girls at once. Who do you think I am? But I'm not going to 'try' anymore," I pouted. "Three girls at once are too much for me. I should have stayed at home to help Dad with the haying."

I made for the stairs and the blissful quiet of my room and locked the door.

# Chapter Three
## The Summer
### 1.

I often wondered, looking back, what would have happened if Rahela Morgan had not invaded my life that long, hot summer of 1989. It's quite probable that I would have fallen in love with Amanda Perkins. I had always been very fond of her and had looked upon her as "my other sister." "She's perfect for you," Dad had told me more than once and I had been half inclined to believe him. But Rahela was in the mix now, and there was no telling what that might mean for all of us.

For a whole week after our trip to the mountains, I avoided Rahela whenever I could. "Dad needs me," was my lame excuse.

"What's wrong?" Kaye demanded one morning over our cup of coffee. "We really don't deserve this."

"There's so much to be done on the farm," I muttered, not meeting her eyes.

"That's not the reason," my twin told me. "You're a coward." And with that, she turned on her heel and stomped out of the room.

That night, we were eating supper and were waiting for Mom to bring in the desert when Dad turned inquisitor, a role I hated immensely.

"What church do you belong to, Rahela?" he asked suddenly. "You've been here several weeks now and I really don't know much about you."

"I'm a member of the Lutheran church," she answered. I could feel myself relaxing. I don't know what answer I had expected, but somehow, not that one.

"So your family is Lutheran?" Dad wanted to know.

Rahela shook her head. "No. It was the nearest church, so we all went there, but my parents never became members. My dad is Eastern Orthodox. He was born Baptist but changed his religion when he married my mother. She was from Romania, you know, so was Romanian orthodox, at least, she became Romanian orthodox. She was originally Christian Brethren."

I glanced at Dad, who, for once in his life, looked completely flummoxed. Even for me, it was a mouthful. Kaye looked puzzled. It was Dad's turn to clear his throat. "And at Rosedale?" he wanted to know. "Have you found a Lutheran church to attend?"

"No, I go to a Pentecostal church near the college," Rahela informed us. She laughed. "I don't know what to think of all the speaking in tongues, but it's a lively, outgoing church and I like that."

"Eastern Orthodox, Lutheran, Pentecostal!" Dad repeated. "Quite a mixture! But I suppose you basically stick to your Lutheran beliefs?"

For a split second, Rahela's eyes met mine, and in that second I realized how nervous she really was. I smiled encouragingly. I knew how intimidating Dad could be. "Actually, Mr. Potter," she began slowly, "my beliefs are in a state of flux right now. When life has thrown you some curveballs before you are mature enough to handle them, it doesn't seem to matter a lot about all these things churches make so much of. Keeping my faith intact is all I can focus on at the moment."

I could see Dad softening. "Thanks for filling us in, Rahela. I hope your time with us will strengthen your faith."

"I hope so too, Mr. Potter."

It was at that moment that I began to understand that this girl sitting opposite me had perhaps seen a lot more of "real" life than I had, though I must have been at least four years older than she. Our eyes met again. What a fool I'd been! The vision of my dreams had landed on my doorstep and I had run away from her! I'd been downright rude. More than that, I'd been a coward instead of a friend.

I knew Dad was watching me, but I didn't care. I felt my lips curving into a broad smile. Rahela smiled back as if to say, "That's better, Mark. What have you been playing at all these days?"

Supper over, Kaye, Rahela, and I sat on the back porch, sipping iced lemonade and listening to the crickets chirp.

"This reminds me of Africa," Rahela said after a few moments of complete silence.

"I'd love to go there," Kaye murmured dreamily. "Life's a bit boring here."

"Africa's a fabulous place," Rahela told us dreamily. "At least, it's fabulous if you like wild, challenging places, with never a day the same. And the nights—they're even more wonderful—full of sounds you never hear anywhere else."

"I'm definitely going with you to Africa," Kaye broke in. "Go on, tell us more."

"You really want to know?" she challenged. We nodded and before we knew it, she had carried us with her to the jungles and plains of Kenya. She made us see the sunsets and stars and the warm, welcoming people. We could almost hear the beat of their drums and sway to the rhythm of their haunting melodies.

"You miss Africa terribly, don't you?" Kaye asked softly when Rahela had finished.

The answer I expected did not come. "I should miss such a fabulous place, shouldn't I?" Rahela's voice had an edge to it. I couldn't follow her mood swing. "Well, I don't really. It holds some…" her voice faltered, "some pretty nasty memories for me." She wasn't smiling now.

Kaye and I exchanged looks. Of course, her mother had died out there in that wild, strange place. But still, I was puzzled.

"I'm sorry to sound so confusing," she apologized. "Africa *is* a fabulous country, but it's also full of danger—poverty, tribal fighting, superstition, cruelty, and ignorance."

My sister gave a shiver. "That doesn't sound very fabulous to me," she muttered.

"But it's my home, Kaye," Rahela reminded her. "I don't think America could ever become my home."

"You're not really happy at Rosedale, are you?" Kaye asked softly.

Rahela didn't answer for a long time. Then she shook her head. "No, not really. I don't fit in anywhere here, not even in church."

We didn't have an answer for that one. Kaye and I were the preachers' kids and were fussed over by all forty or fifty members of the church we looked on as our second home.

"It'll take time," Kaye said after a long pause. "Adjusting always takes time."

Rahela shrugged and said nothing.

"I don't know why Kaye is so taken with Rahela," Dad confided the next morning as we sipped our cups of steaming coffee. We had always been the early risers in the house and it seemed it was still that way.

"Kaye's a pretty good judge of character, Dad, you know that," I reminded him. I was a bit upset by his comment.

"Rahela seems a really mixed-up kid," he went on. "Maybe we can help her sort herself out, spiritually, I mean."

I got up from the bar stool and made for the door. "Just because she's different, Dad, doesn't mean she's mixed up," I protested.

"Well, but Lutheran, Orthodox, Pentecostal? She doesn't even know what she believes! Mark. So what does it all add up to?"

I shrugged. "Don't know and honestly couldn't care. If she loves God, isn't that all that matters?"

My father grimaced a little. "Yes, *if* she loves God. But does she?"

I'd had enough. What was up with my father? "You have it in for Rahela Morgan," I exploded. "I can only suppose I'm at the bottom of it. You're worried that I'll fall for her, aren't you? That's the only thing that makes sense of your prejudice against Rahela."

Dad reddened. Then he put a hand on my arm and said in a much gentler tone, "It's so important whom you marry. Rahela is a dark-horse. Be careful. Next to knowing God, picking a wife is the most important thing you will ever do."

"I know Dad, and I appreciate your concern. But I'm not about to marry Rahela Morgan."

"Good." He scratched his head as he went on slowly. "I can't put it into words but Rahela's different. I'm not sure about her Christianity."

"Sometimes I'm not even sure about mine!" It was out before I could stop it.

That didn't sound good, coming from a Bible college graduate. Dad looked shocked, but only for a split second. I felt his hand on my shoulder. "It's God you need to be sure about, Mark, not Christianity." The obvious pity in his tone made me flinch. "And you are sure of *Him*, aren't you?"

Sure of God? What did that mean? Sure He existed? Of course. Sure He loved me? Yes. But suddenly Rahela's words that evening came back to me: "Actually, when you've faced certain things in life.....keeping your faith intact is all you can focus on at the moment." What had *I* faced, I wondered?

Dad was waiting for an answer. "I'm sure right now," I told him, weighing each word carefully, "but would I be so sure if my world was suddenly turned upside down? I suppose I'll have to wait and see."

"You disappoint me, Mark," was all Dad said.

It wasn't the first time I'd heard that remark. "Need to go, Dad," I muttered and left the room.

## 2.

I will never forget my third Sunday home. My first had been spent at Amanda's church. Her dad was pastor and there was a missionary from Kenya speaking so we had all been invited. I noticed Rahela hadn't been that impressed. Nor was I, for that matter. The second Sunday I had come down with a very heavy cold and decided to stay home. Now, at last, I was returning to the church I had been raised in. The choir director was having surgery and Kaye had wheedled Dad into inviting Rahela to provide the special music.

"She has a fabulous voice," Kaye told me as we walked the quarter mile walk to the church. "Her mother was an opera singer."

"Is she nervous, do you think?"

Kaye shook her head. "I don't think so. She's used to singing in public; says it's second nature. Listen. She's going over her song now with Mom."

We were still some distance from the church, but I could hear every word and every note of "Amazing Grace" wafting through the open door.

"Angelic!" Kaye murmured. "And she sings as if she means it."

I raised my eyebrows. "Isn't that what you would expect from Rahela?"

Kaye shrugged. "I suppose so, though Dad wouldn't agree."

"Dad is wary of her brand of Christianity, whatever that is."

Kaye gave me a knowing look. "He can't label her, Mark. That's the problem."

I frowned. "Why should he?"

"In order to cope with her. To begin with, remember what she told him the other night—parents Eastern Orthodox who attended a Lutheran church most of Rahela's childhood?"

"Remember?" I repeated grinning. "How could I ever forget the look on Dad's face! Well then, can you label *me*?" I wanted to know.

"Sure. That's easy," Kaye said, a bit too cockily. "Mark Potter—loyal citizen of the United States of America, Republican, Independent Evangelical, patriotic, is against gun control, global warming, women pastors, is a six day creationist. In short, knows what he believes religiously and politically and is sure of God and his salvation."

"Finished?" I asked as we had reached the door of the church. It was obviously time to stop the conversation.

"No way," Kaye whispered. "I haven't touched on what you believe about abortion, same sex marriage, closing our borders, courtship, raising a family, fighting for your country..."

"Stop it," I warned. "You make me sound terribly predictable."

"Well, aren't you?" Kaye wanted to know as we slipped into our usual seat.

I didn't answer. I thought of what I'd told Dad a few days ago. Kaye didn't know that I was far more unsure of myself than I let on.

I watched as Rahela whispered a few words to Mom at the piano and then made her way to our pew.

"Sit here," Kaye told her, "between the Potter twins. Mark and I talk too much when we're together."

Rahela blushed, hesitated for just a second or two, and then took the proffered seat. Meanwhile, I was trying to do something Dad had failed to do, label her! Christian, yes, I was pretty sure of that but what kind I couldn't tell for the life of me. Dad was right in that. And politically—I hadn't a clue. But that wouldn't be for long. A whole summer with a girl would surely enable me to figure out who she was.

"What else do you do besides singing like an angel?" I whispered as the church began to fill up.

Rahela blushed furiously then shrugged. "Oh, I play the piano and organ and..." She stopped short and blushed again.

"She's too modest to catalog all her accomplishments," Kaye interrupted. "She also plays the guitar, piano accordion, and flute; knows Romanian, Latin, French, and Swahili; loves to write poetry and compose songs. But she's not much good at tennis; can't swim very well; isn't much good at art, and doesn't like to speak in public. There, see how well I've gotten to know her?"

Dad's voice broke into our conversation. "We will open our service this morning by singing hymn no. 456."

As I'd expected, Rahela wowed everyone by her solo. Even Dad was spellbound. It may have even inspired him to outdo himself that morning as he spoke eloquently on "That I may know Him," from Philippians 2. The altar call was more prolonged than usual and the front rail was filled with kneeling figures before we had reached the last stanza of "Just as I am."

Rahela seemed unusually quiet as we walked home after the service. "I've a bit of a headache," she explained after lunch as she went up to her room and stayed there until time for the evening service.

"Give us your testimony, Rahela," Dad suggested, as we sat sipped hot chocolate and munched on Mom's oatmeal and raisin cookies after church that evening. I thought that it was totally unfair of him to put her on the spot like that in front of Amanda and Reg and other church friends.

"Testimony?" Rahela repeated, somewhat puzzled.

"Yes, tell us how you came to know Christ personally."

Rahela blushed scarlet. "You mean do it now, just like that?"

Dad nodded. There was a long silence. Then Rahela cleared her throat. "Mr. Potter," she began, "what would you feel like if I invited you to my home, gathered some friends together, and then asked you to tell people you didn't know very well about your intimate relationship with your wife?"

A gasp went around the room followed by a long, awkward silence. It took my usually resourceful father a very long time to come to his senses, master his feelings, and reply as calmly as he could: "Your analogy doesn't hold, Rahela. And even if it did, I'd be glad to tell anyone how I met my wife. I am not asking you to read us your spiritual diary, only to tell us how you first came to know the Savior."

"But I can't, Mr. Potter. Please don't ask me to do the impossible." It was clear to me that Rahela was on the verge of tears.

"That's enough, Dad," I said rising from my chair. "Testimonies shouldn't be forced, should they?"

Dad's face was a picture. I couldn't think of the last time I'd countered him in public. As for Rahela, it was impossible to tell if she was glad I had intervened nor not. I only know that I was totally unprepared for what she said next.

"It's not that I haven't met Christ, Mr. Potter," she explained slowly. "It's that the encounter with Him was so overpowering that I can't talk about it, especially not in a group like this."

Dad's face was a picture. I suppose mine was too. Then Mom took control. "Time for refreshments," she announced. "Kaye, Rahela, maybe you could both give me a hand in the kitchen for a few moments?"

The rest of the evening was uneventful. I managed to snatch a few words with Rahela when everyone had left. "Sorry about what happened," I apologized. "Dad's used to commanding us all."

"Don't be sorry," she murmured. "It's me. I don't fit in anywhere here in America."

I started to remonstrate, but she was gone. I lay awake for what seemed hours that night, thinking about Rahela, of course. Who else? She had captivated me from the start. And I was fooling myself. I had never believed much in the "soul mate" theory. It was too idealistic. But now I wasn't so sure. If anyone was my soul mate, it was this Welsh-Romanian who had blown into my life that cold, chilly December day and was already dispersing a few ancient cobwebs.

Just past two that morning, I was awakened out of a deep sleep by a scream coming from Kaye's bedroom. I jumped out of bed, grabbed my dressing-gown, and sprinted up the hallway. Mom had beaten me to it and was tapping on Kaye's door.

"Everything OK?" she wanted to know.

The door opened slightly. "Rahela had a nightmare," Kaye whispered. "She's OK now."

Mom and I looked at each other. "That girl's gone through something or other that she's told very few about, Mark," she confided as we walked slowly back to our rooms.

I didn't feel like discussing Rahela with anyone right then.

Rahela didn't come down to breakfast the next morning. "She's worn out and a bit ashamed of wakening the whole house last night," Kaye told us. "She went through an awful experience about three or four years ago and she's never been the same since. Every so often, she relives it in horrible nightmares."

From the way Kaye glanced at me, I suspected Rahela had told her a lot more than that.

"How awful, Kaye. The poor child!" Mom exclaimed. "I'm so glad she's spending some time with us."

"Yes, it seems very providential," Dad agreed.

"You didn't tell us the half, did you?" I asked Kaye when we were washing up the dishes.

"Of course not," Kaye retorted, slipping her arm around me. "It's confidential, Mark. Even twins have secrets sometimes." She was smiling as she spoke but something in her eyes told me that those "secrets" had been pretty deep ones. And there and then, I made up my mind that I, too, would become the kind of friend Rahela could trust with her secrets.

## 3

About three weeks after my return home, Amanda and her brother went on their annual family vacation. With them both out of the picture for a while at least, I had no hesitation in joining Kaye and Rahela on their daily jaunts. Knoxville, the lake, and the mountains—I drove them everywhere and anywhere. Kaye was always our chaperone, at least that's what it turned out to be: Rahela and I in the front, and my good, dutiful twin in the back.

Two weeks fled by, and then Amanda and her brother returned. Their presence certainly made things a little more awkward but, just then, Dad decided he needed me to help him to harvest another field of hay. There were still the evenings, though, when we'd play games together, or go for strolls by the river, or play tennis, or have a musical evening. Rahela, Kaye, Reg, and I formed a quartet with Amanda playing the piano.

Rahela stayed with us nearly three whole months. As the days passed, I hoped Dad would soften towards the "foreign girl," but, instead, he became visibly worried. Predictable, trustworthy Amanda was fading into the background while this mysterious stranger was slowly but surely taking her place. At least that's how he would put it. I knew differently. No one else had ever occupied the place Rahela now held in my life.

Summer was almost over so what was next? Did I go my way and she hers, trusting providence to throw us together at some point in the future? Was that likely? Did such things happen more than twice in a life time?

"Make the best of these last few weeks," a Voice whispered, whether providence, God, or just my own gut feelings, I'm not sure. Maybe all three rolled into one. Anyway, I followed the Voice's advice that very afternoon and took Rahela out for a long drive into the mountains. For the first time, we were just the two of us. I knew it needed to be that way.

We had paused for a picnic lunch at a rest area. The view was breathtaking, the weather superb, and Rahela, for once, seemed perfectly relaxed.

"It's so good not to have to talk all the time," she breathed.

I nodded, grinning. "It doesn't always take words to communicate," I said.

"Not with someone who understands you!"

I smiled. That was a compliment all right, but not completely true. "I understand what I know about you, Rahela," I told her, "but I can't understand what I don't know. And that's still quite a lot."

"What more do you want to know, Mark?" she asked as we made our way to a bench and sat down. "I've told you about growing up in Africa, about Mother's dying, about my dreams for the future, haven't I?"

I nodded. "Yes. But I feel I don't really know who you are, Rahela."

"Meaning?"

Now she really was putting me on the spot. "Well...." I stammered. I knew I had to be absolutely honest with her. "You seem to be hiding something, Rahela," I told her, meeting her gaze.

She reddened and dropped her eyes. "Don't we all hide things from each other, even from close friends, Mark?"

"Yes," I conceded, "though the closer you are to someone the more you tell them, don't you? And I really do want to be...."

I stopped abruptly. What did I want to be to this girl?

"Well then, Mark," she said softly, "when our friendship reaches whatever level you were meaning, if it ever does, then I promise I won't hide a thing from you."

We were both beating about the bush and we knew it. I began again: "Look, Rahela," we've gotten pretty close during the past few weeks, but what happens now partly depends on what trust we can have in each other, doesn't it?"

"I've been through a lot, Mark," she said softly. "It'll take me a long time to learn to completely trust anyone again." She gazed out over the mountains and seemed to gain courage. "I was brutally raped when I was seventeen, just two years after mother died," she blurted out, burying her face in her hands.

I squeezed her hand tight. Somehow, I wasn't shocked. Nightmares? Something terrible had happened, Kaye had said? It all made sense.

"You're not shocked?" she wanted to know.

I took her hand in mine and held it tightly. "No, I'm not. And it doesn't make any difference to me, Rahela. Not one bit!"

The look of relief on her face was just too much for me. I took her in my arms, then, and told her I loved her.

"I love you too, Mark," she said. And I knew she meant it.

After that trip to the mountains, we both threw caution to the winds. It was obvious to everyone that we were in love. We spent every spare moment alone together, and how we talked! Rahela told me what she believed, and I told her what I believed. We agreed in some things and differed in others. That was normal, or so I persuaded myself. I was walking on air, assured that the girl of my dreams was becoming the love of my life.

Then, one evening towards the end of July, Mom and Dad invited Amanda's family over for a barbecue. Kaye's boyfriend, Tom, had just returned home for his tour in Iraq so he was there, too. He was a great guy and we all loved him almost as much as Kaye did!

After we had made gluttons of ourselves, at least Tom and I had, we leaned back in our deckchairs for an after-supper chat. The news' headlines for the past few days had focused on several shootouts and so, of course, the topic of the day soon came up—gun control. Something had to be done, we all agreed. Problem was: what?

My dad, Amanda's dad and her brother Reg soon waxed eloquent on the subject. I glanced over at Rahela. She and Kaye were deep in some conversation of their own.

"Good," I thought. I knew what Rahela believed on the subject and hoped she wasn't listening. Fond hope!

Dad was making it quite clear that any tightening on gun control would absolutely violate our rights as American citizens. "The government is trying to take away our Fifth Amendment rights," he thundered. "It's disgraceful! We Christians need to speak out, loud and clear; otherwise they'll keep decent folk from defending themselves and put weapons into the hands of evil men. And in the end, our country will be totally destroyed." Dad paused for breath, giving Amanda's father time to get his word in.

"I suppose if Peter had been living today," he interjected, "he would have been asked for a background check before he could use his sword to defend our Lord in the garden of Gethsemane," and he gave a hearty chuckle, feeling he had made a very clever and valid point.

Rahela stopped talking to Kaye and turned around to face us. "But, Mr. Perkins," she interrupted, "have you forgotten Jesus' reaction to Peter's sword-play? I think He told him to put his weapon away, didn't he?"

Rahela's words struck us all as a bolt from the blue and left us speechless. "And," she went on, "on another occasion, didn't Jesus make the statement, 'Those who use the sword will perish with the sword'?"

There was a dead silence. No one answered Rahela. She had obviously flummoxed two pastors and one potential pastor with two brief questions. I suddenly felt very proud of her, although I didn't agree with her on gun control, so how could I defend her? We had already differed about it up there on the mountain some weeks previously.

"We'll be eaten alive if we stay outside one minute longer," Mom announced suddenly, swooping up a pile of empty paper plates and depositing them with great gusto into the trash can nearby.

Soon, our guests had gone and Rahela had excused herself saying she had a headache. I tried to sneak off to bed before Dad could buttonhole me as I had a feeling he certainly would if he got a chance. But it was no use.

"I want a word with you, Mark," he told me in his lecturing voice. I stifled a groan and followed him obediently into the front parlor. He closed the door, sat down, and cleared his throat.

"I hope you aren't getting too fond of that foreign girl, Mark," he said solemnly. "She showed her true colors tonight, didn't she?"

"What do you mean, Dad?" I wouldn't give him one inch if I could help it.

"Oh, come on," he said exasperatedly. "You know as well as I do that she was impudent, brazen, and of course, very wrong."

"No, I don't know that," I exploded. "Rahela Morgan is never impudent or brazen. She might be wrong in some of her beliefs; I agree on that. But Greg Perkins asked for what he got tonight, didn't he?"

Dad looked taken aback. "Well, Greg often sticks his foot in things. He didn't exactly use an appropriate scripture to defend gun rights. But he was on the right side. Rahela isn't. You know that, Mark."

The right side? Well, it certainly was the side I'd been on for as long as I could remember. But he had been unfair, very unfair on Rahela, and I told him that in no uncertain terms.

"You should have said something on the patio," a small voice whispered as I got ready for bed that night. "You were a coward."

I couldn't answer that one. I knew it was true. I couldn't have defended Rahela's point of view maybe, but I could have defended the girl behind that point of view just as I had done to Dad in private.

I told that to Rahela early the next morning. It was Sunday and we were grabbing a light breakfast before setting out on the quarter of a mile walk to our church. "It's Ok, Mark," she told me. "I put my foot in it. I'll watch my mouth next time."

And she tried in the days which followed, but it wasn't much use. Dad's suspicions had been aroused. He had to discover exactly what this "foreign girl" believed. At every possible opportunity, Dad would waylay her and quiz her. Did she believe you could lose your salvation? Did she believe in women preachers? Did she believe in global warming? Did she think the world was created in six literal days? And as her answers never quite meshed with his, no, more than that, quite often contradicted his beliefs, things went from bad to worse.

"Only another week, so hang in there," Kaye told her one evening when we three were alone together.

"Is it that bad?" I wanted to know. I'd tried to make up for Dad's attitude by spending more and more time with her. I had thought that would compensate, but maybe it hadn't.

"Dad's pretty tough on her, you know that," Kaye told me, a glint in her sky blue eyes. "If only he would leave her alone and we could go back a few weeks, before that awful barbeque."

"You've been so kind, Kaye," Rahela interjected. "You, too, Mark. And your Mom. And even…"

"Don't try to explain Dad away," I interrupted. "He means well but he's been downright rude at times."

"Well, he knows what I've told you both more than once," Rahela said. "I simply don't fit in here."

"Maybe not with him," I protested, "but with me, and with Kaye, well, you've fit in pretty well, to put it mildly."

Rahela blushed. "I know. That's the problem," she said quietly.

That last week I tried to get time alone with Rahela, but she made it as difficult as she possibly could. I became frustrated, then angry, until Kaye took me aside and said gently, "Listen, Mark, Rahela knows you're both getting extremely fond of each other and sees no way that anything can work out between you."

"Why ever not?" I exploded.

"She says that, even apart from Dad, she wouldn't really fit into your life."

"Rubbish!" I exploded again. "We've a lot in common, and you know it," I told my twin.

"Yes, but you are a declared Republican and a fundamentalist evangelical, while she's neither." Kaye retorted. "So what about church, and friends, and yes, Dad?"

"You told me we were soul mates," I reminded her. "So what's the problem?"

Kaye gave me one of her special hugs. "Well, if you really are soul mates," she whispered, "then, one day, you'll come together again, won't you?"

Later I was to remember her words, but at the time they merely riled me. I was too angry, too frustrated, too confused to listen. It was all right for Kaye. She'd be married soon to a good, steady guy, who measured up to all our expectations and then some, while I was in love with some mysterious phantom, who wafted in and out of my life at will, leaving me grasping at a shadow.

"Don't write to me, Mark," Rahela told me as we said good bye a few days later.

"Of course I'll write," I told her. "We love each other, Rahela." She didn't try to counter that. She couldn't. But she wouldn't let me take her in my arms again. "Forget about me," she whispered as Kaye appeared on the doorstep ready to drive her to college. "It's been a great summer. But we're not suited, Mark. It just won't work."

I stood and watched Kaye's car turn onto the main road and disappear. I heard Mom breathe a sigh of relief and saw the triumphant expression on Dad's face and I lost it, I mean totally lost it. I told them both just what I thought of them and their religion, told them I'd never marry anyone else. And then I turned and saw Amanda coming towards our house—safe, beautiful Amanda, saw her smile, recognized love in her eyes, and I hesitated. Maybe they were all right. Maybe Rahela wasn't for me, never had been. Maybe providence had played me tricks twice and I couldn't trust it anymore.

"Sorry, I blew it," I apologized.

"I understand why you're so upset," Mom said, patting my arm. "Give yourself time, Mark. You'll get over this, believe me you will."

For a few moments, maybe a few hours, I believed her, but that was all. Alone that night, I felt I'd never ever get over Rahela Morgan.

Dad called me into his office a few days after she and Kaye had left for college. I listened silently to a catalog of Rahela's erroneous beliefs, determined not to blow it again. But I knew already exactly what she believed. I had heard all this from her own lips. And what Dad was not cataloging was all the things she believed in that we believed in too—the essentials of our faith. What we agreed on seemed so important that what we didn't faded into insignificance.

And, to give Dad his dues, he might have thought the same thing, if Rahela had been simply a friend of Kaye's. But she wasn't. He knew, and Rev. Perkins knew, and Amanda knew, and Mom knew, and most of all, Kaye knew that Rahela was the girl Mark Potter, son of Pastor Potter, graduate of Swansea Bible College, had fallen for. That was where the snag lay. Sure, Rahela could be mixed up and unorthodox and maybe squeeze into Heaven one day if she believed in Christ, but to perhaps become the wife of future pastor Mark Potter—that was a totally different story!

In the hours and days which followed Rahela's departure, I desperately tried to sort things out in my own mind. I blamed Amanda's dad, blamed my dad, blamed Mum, and then, after a lot of heart-searching and many talks with my forthright twin, I turned inward and discovered I had been in love with the idea of Rahela more than with Rahela herself. I'd forget her and hope she did the same with me.

Anyway, what did it matter? It was highly unlikely I'd ever see her again. Kaye told me later that she had only seen Rahela once since their return to college. She had looked her up at Rosedale one weekend. Rahela had been friendly enough, but it had been obvious she didn't want to get too close. Yes, she was doing fine. Everyone spoke highly of her. No, she didn't seem to be pining for me though she sent her regards.

"She doesn't seem to want another boyfriend, though," Kaye told me. "I think you spoiled her for anyone else."

I entered Vanderbilt that fall and, though I pushed Rahela to the very back of my mind, I had to admit that she had changed me forever. Try as I would, I couldn't go back to being the Mark Potter I used to be. I began to question lots of things. Rahela had somehow dragged me into a gray zone where there were often no cut and dried answers to life's dilemmas. I still called myself Republican, and my friends obviously considered me pretty much a fundamentalist, but inside, where it really counted, I was in turmoil. At times, Amanda seemed the answer—a good steady girlfriend would bring me back to my senses, Dad repeatedly told me. But it was no use. For better or for worse, Rahela Morgan had changed me forever!

# Chapter Four
# Third Impressions
## 1.

Life at Vanderbilt suited me to a T. I loved my studies, respected my professors, and liked the church I attended. And then, at the end of my second year, I met a great guy at church called Luke Gryson, a fine Christian who was hoping to be a missionary doctor one day. We got on so well, we decided to share an apartment in the fall.

That summer, Mom did her best to persuade me that Amanda was the girl for me. And I began to wonder if maybe she was right. She had matured a lot and was, of course, as attractive as ever. She'd certainly help to keep me steady. So we spent a lot of time together but, somehow, that's as far as it went.

"Write to me Mark," she said, as I left for school that fall.

I hesitated. "Please," she begged. "I miss you so much when you leave."

"OK," I promised. "I'll write."

And I did. Amanda was a wonderful letter-writer and I began to look forward to her epistles, for that's what they were.

"Girlfriend?" Luke asked as he handed me an envelope in her familiar handwriting.

I shrugged. "Not quite," I explained. "At least, not yet. Maybe never. To tell you the truth, Luke, I've been spoiled."

Luke grinned. "So it's like that, is it? Tell me about *her* unless it's too painful."

I shook my head. "No, it didn't go that far. But still, no one ever seems to come up to her."

"Name?"

Luke said later, he didn't know why he became so curious. It wasn't really like him. Not that I minded. So I said simply, "Rahela. That's her name. Romanian actually. She was half Romanian, half Welsh. And I tell you Luke, she was something else."

Just uttering her name had swept me back two years to that memorable summer when the "foreign girl" had invaded my life. I was so lost in memories that I was not aware of the affect her name had had on Luke until I heard him muttering, "I can't believe it! Talk about providence! Rahela Morgan of all people!"

I jumped up from my chair and grabbed his sleeve. "What are you muttering about, Luke. You know her—know Rahela? This can't be happening. Not three times in a row!"

Luke took me by the arm and sat me down again. "Now calm down, Mark," he told me. "And yes, I think I know this girl, but first, tell me all about her, that is, if you don't mind."

Mind? Of course I didn't mind. So I spilled it all out, right from the beginning, lost label and all.

"That's Rahela all right," he said slowly when I'd finished. "We med students have a Christian fellowship every week and I met her there when school started again this year. It's her first year so I tried to make her feel welcome, show her the ropes. She was gracious but a bit stand-offish—didn't seem to fit in too well in our fellowship. But I took to her, though, and asked her out. She refused, of course."

Luke paused a moment. "Why of course?" I asked, tongue in cheek.

"For the same reason as you gave a moment ago—she's spoiled."

I gave a short laugh and shook my head. "I doubt it, but you're sure it's the same girl?"

Luke said nothing but walked over to his desk and pulled out a note book. He turned the pages and then handed the book to me. Pointing to a name halfway down the page he said, "There's her number. You can soon find out if it's the same girl."

"No way," I retorted. "She'll never look at me again after the way my dad treated her."

"Listen to me, will you?" Luke said almost fiercely and very uncharacteristically. "What do you think God is doing with you? Playing a game, or trying to get your attention? Third time round, if you let her go, she'll probably be gone forever. Go after her, man."

"But she…"

"Go after her," he repeated. "Here's her phone number. Now grab at this providence with both hands. And if it doesn't work out, then you won't be spending all your life regretting something you didn't do but could have done."

"I'll think about it," I promised, which I did for about half an hour until, finally, I grabbed the phone, dialed the number Luke and given me, and waited.

"Rahela?" I asked as I heard a voice answering on the other end.

Dead silence. "Rahela?" I repeated. "It's me, Mark. I know this is a surprise, but Luke Gryson gave me your phone number." Still no answer, but at least she hadn't hung up on me.

"Rahela?" I said once more, determined not to be put off by her silence. "I'm coming over to see you. I'll meet you in the cafeteria. If you absolutely don't want anything to do with me, then send a message with your roommate. But as Luke reminded me, either the Almighty is playing with us, which I very much doubt, or…."

"I'll be there," I heard her mutter. Then the receiver went click. I looked at Luke who was grinning like a Cheshire cat.

"Pray, please," I begged as I grabbed my sweater and car keys.

"Sure will," was his answer. "My, but this is something else, Mark. Talk about real life being stranger than fiction."

"The story isn't over," I reminded him.

"You bet it isn't," Luke said with a wink. "I'll stay up till you get home."

"I'll be back before too long," I assured him, as I made for the door. "I don't think she's keen to see me."

I'll never forget that ride to the campus cafeteria. I was a bundle of nerves. What was I doing, or rather God doing? One thing I knew. I'd take it real easy. And this time I'd insist on getting to know the real Rahela Morgan, if she gave me half a chance, that is."

But all my resolutions fled the moment I saw her, sitting alone at a table near the front of the cafeteria. She rose when she saw me. No, she didn't fly into my arms. Instead, she said, very deliberately as we walked slowly towards each other: "Mark, I can't take a repeat of what happened that summer. I really can't. I haven't changed in what I think and believe in. And I don't suppose you have either. So why...."

I put up my hand to stop her. "You and I both know what the problem was, Rahela," I said firmly. "It wasn't our beliefs. We agree on the things that matter."

"But your dad," she interrupted. "He'd never change."

"Maybe not. But if....," I stopped. How could I put it? I hadn't seen her for two years so how could I talk about love and marriage?

Our eyes met and in that instant, the past two years melted away. "I need a friend here, Mark," Rahela whispered. "I'm lonely and everything's new. It seems God has sent you along. But at least till Christmas, let's just be friends—getting to know each other, and I mean really knowing each other, right?"

I nodded. And it dawned on me that, even on that glorious day in the mountains, we had discussed our beliefs in detail, but sharing our lives, our thoughts, our fears? No we hadn't done that. And that's what real friends do.

"OK," I agreed, just friends till Christmas."

Rahela sat down, relieved. "Then could you get me a coffee, please?" she asked coyly. "And make it strong. I've an exam tomorrow."

"Then I shouldn't be taking your time," I protested.

"I need a break," she reassured me. "So, coffee, please."

By the time the hour was up, I realized Rahela had changed a lot. She was infinitely more mature and not as serious. Maybe it was because we didn't have Dad breathing down our necks. Maybe it was because we were just being "friends." Who knew why, but whatever the reason, I liked what was happening between us.

"See you soon?" I asked as she rose to go.

"This Friday?" she suggested.

"This Friday," I agreed.

"God," I prayed that night, "I don't know what you're doing, but Luke's right; I need to take advantage of whatever it is. And if Rahela isn't the girl for me, then before Christmas, please Lord, make it plain." And with that, I rolled into bed and slept like a baby.

"I was afraid you'd never look at me again," I told her over a Subway sandwich that Friday afternoon. I'd thought a lot during the past two days and was pretty certain she had too.

"Why on earth did you think that?" she wanted to know.

"My father treated you abominably."

"But that wasn't your fault, Mark."

I smiled. "Maybe not, but…"

"No buts," she interrupted. "It had to be that way. So, are you ready for what you'll find out, about me?"

"Sure. I'm ready for everything."

"You just don't know what you're saying Mark."

"You're still hiding something from me," I wanted to tell her and then, just in time, bit my words and reminded myself that of course she was keeping something from me. I didn't really know her. Why wouldn't she have some secrets she wasn't ready to share with me! Well, I had till Christmas. You can learn a lot about someone in three whole months.

And so, every weekend, we'd get together. Sometimes we'd hike—she loved that—or play tennis, she loved that even more, or go to concerts—that, too, was a favorite. Well, was there anything she didn't like to do with me? Not really, except attend the church near the college where I had been going for two years.

"I don't fit in there, Mark," she told me more than once.

And so we looked for one which suited us both and found a Methodist church which did that pretty well, for the most part. Dad about died when he heard where I was attending, but I was always giving him near death experiences, more or less. I had refused to go to seminary and instead, was well on the way to becoming a vet. He didn't know, as yet, that I'd taken up with Rahela. Luke called our friendship serious dating, but I'd never admit that. What I did admit freely to anyone who would listen was this: there was just no one like her—no one as interesting or as genuine as Rahela Morgan.

"So you think I am a real Christian, Mark?" she asked me one night as we sat eating supper in our favorite restaurant.

"Yes, of course I do," I answered, grinning.

"When did you come to that conclusion?"

I thought a moment before answering. "Just being with you convinces me of that," I said. "Only I wish you'd tell me more about how you came to be one."

"I came to know Christ personally after I was raped, Mark."

I thought of that evening Dad had tried to force Rahela into giving her testimony and of her response. "Tell me more, Rahela," I told her.

"Well, I'd gone to church before that, but much of what I heard went over my head. But when I felt spoiled and soiled, I imagined no one would ever love me again, except Dad of course. Then, my nurse, Deborah, took me in my arms one night when I had one of those awful nightmares and led me to Christ. I really seemed to meet him, Mark. She told me He would wash me clean and He did. I felt so close to Him for weeks after that. His love overwhelmed me."

All I could do was stare down into her eyes and try to imagine what she had suffered.

Then she was in my arms. "Poor, poor Rahela," I whispered. "No wonder you didn't want to give your "testimony" that evening.

She was sobbing into my chest now. "Want to tell me more?" I whispered.

She shook her head. "Not now, Mark. Someday, I promise," she answered quickly. "That is, if we decide….." She didn't need to finish. I'd already made my decision but wasn't quite sure she had.

That evening marked a turning point in our relationship. Our friendship took on new meaning. I began to share my hopes and fears with her.

Mid-term arrived before we knew it. I decided to take Rahela to Atlanta to visit my aunt. My parents must have been puzzled but they said little. After all, they had always encouraged me to spend time with my spinster aunt.

Rahela and I spent a wonderful weekend together. Aunt Anna fell in love with her instantly. Thanksgiving, however, was another matter. Rahela insisted on going to some friends of her father's in Raleigh. She couldn't face spending even a few days with our family—couldn't face Dad, not just yet.

So I went home and shared my secret with Kaye who was ecstatic. "See, I told you," she reminded me. "Once soul mates, always soul mates."

## 2.

I went back to Vanderbilt, counting the days till Christmas. "Let's spend it at my aunt's in Atlanta," I suggested.

Rahela shook her head. "No, you need to be with your family. But what about New Year?"

That sounded reasonable. "And New Year's Eve, I'll tell you everything," Rahela promised.

Christmas, for once in my life, dragged on interminably. Dad was furious when he found out that I'd gotten back with Rahela.

"Why does it need to be her, Mark?" he complained.

"Because she's the best thing that ever happened to me, Dad," I said simply.

"Even though she's a liberal, Mark? I mean, how can two walk together if they're not agreed? Have you forgotten that?"

I felt anger flowing through every part of me. "A liberal!" I exploded. "You hardly know anything about her. I do. She's no more a real liberal than you or I."

"What about her views on abortion, then, or women's rights, or....?"

"We agree on some and disagree on others. But we're both Christians, Dad. We've got so much in common, and I know she's not a liberal. She doesn't talk like one, worship like one, or pray like one."

"At least you're not engaged?" he wanted to know.

"Not yet."

Dad gripped my hand. "Listen, son. Promise me you'll find out all you need to know about her before you make your final decision. She's such a dark horse. Do it, please, for all our sakes, promise?"

I hesitated just one moment and then said firmly, "I promise."

And so I left for Great Aunt Anna's, knowing instinctively that, come New Year, my fate would be decided. We only had a few days together so I knew that, sooner rather than later, we'd have to make our decision, or, as far as I was concerned, own up to the decision I had already made. Three months of "being friends" had convinced me that, no matter what I might discover about Rahela Morgan, she was the woman for me. I'd take her and cherish her, for better or for worse, for the rest of my days.

We were eating breakfast together in Auntie's kitchen the morning after Rahela's arrival. Aunt Anna had turned on the TV. Some guy running for reelection in a governor's race was speaking about abortion.

"And do you make exception in the case of pregnancy as a result of a rape?" the reporter asked.

"Well," the man began, "I think that while rape is a horrible crime, any life given even through such a crime, comes from God and is His will."

I stared at the screen in disbelief at the man's insensibility. And then I heard her, Rahela, I mean. She had risen from her seat and had marched right up to the TV.

"You insensitive idiot," she yelled. Yes, she was literally yelling. I'd never heard her do that before. "You liar!"

I grabbed her arm. "Rahela," I pleaded. "Calm down!"

"But Mark, didn't you hear what he said?"

"I heard him. He opened his mouth and put his foot in it."

"Is that all you can say? He's rude, unfeeling, and…."

She stopped for breath. "What he meant to say," I explained, "was that God is the author of all life, Rahela, and so that life is precious. But it didn't come out right."

"I'll say it didn't!" Rahela exploded. "He pretty much said that a child born as a result of rape was God's will."

"He's…" I began.

"He's a Republican," she shot back. "That's what he is. He's one of your dad's good Christian gentlemen."

And then, suddenly, she shook herself clear of me and bolted out the door. I was after her in a flash.

"Leave her, Mark," Aunt Anna commanded. She sounded more like a sergeant major than my gentle little aunt. "Let her be. Give her time."

And then it hit me. This must have something to do with her "dark secret"—the fear in her eyes that I've never understood. It must be something to do with….

I started to shake all over. Aunt Anna came up to me. I felt her hand on my arm. "Trust her, Mark. And don't prejudge. Listen to her story and then cover it with all the love you have."

"I thought I already knew her story," I spluttered.

"It's obvious you don't, isn't it?"

A few hours later, we were sitting in a park nearby, and Rahela was talking at last. It all came pouring out like a fountain.

"It happened a few years before I met you in Wales," she began. "I...I...."

"Look, if this is too much for you...."

"It *is* too much, but I've got to do it Mark. Make it easy for me, please."

"How?" I wanted to know.

"By listening. Don't interrupt even when I shock you, right?"

"Right," I promised, my chest tightening.

So she told me...everything. How her dad was usually so careful at leaving her alone on the plantation. He had reason to be. There was a guy who used to work for him who had always had his eyes on his daughter, ever since she had been a girl of fourteen. But, as far as everyone knew, he was in prison in faraway Johannesburg. Only, he had been released on bail and no one on the Morgan plantation knew anything about it. That was why Rahela's dad thought it was Ok to leave her alone one morning with just her maid Deborah, when he was called away suddenly. One of his workers had had a near fatal accident, he was told. Only he hadn't. It was all set up by Rahela's attacker who soon overpowered Deborah and did his worst to Rahela. Two months later, Rahela realized that she was pregnant. She had felt like committing suicide when she discovered the truth.

My heart broke as I listened. "You've no idea what I felt, Mark," she sobbed as I held her tight. "I knew the child would be half of h-i-m! I had dreaded him for years. I'd had nightmares about him, had visions of his face at night—and now, he was the father of my child. I'd have to see his face reflected in him, (I was sure it would be a boy) every day of my life. What if I brought a demon into the world who would torture others as his father had tortured me? No, I couldn't, I wouldn't do it!"

She stopped speaking and laid her head on my shoulder. I thought I knew what was coming and held my breath. "I obviously didn't commit suicide," Rahela went on. "Instead, I had an abortion."

In our family that word was practically taboo. I couldn't believe my ears. I had prepared myself for nearly everything that Rahela might tell me but not for this.

Rahela was staring away now into space and couldn't see my face. "Dad plead with me for hours not to do it," she told me, "but he finally said I must do what I felt was right. It was I, not he, who would have to live with my conscience forever."

Her story was finally over. Rahela had kept her eyes fixed on the ground as she told her tragic tale. But now, timidly, she lifted them to mine to read my reaction. I went frantic. An abortion! A life snuffed out just like that! A murder! That's what I'd been taught all my life. And yet….could I blame her? No, not blame her. I couldn't do that. But the question went deeper. Could I still think of her as my future wife?

I'll never forget what followed. For just one moment I avoided her gaze. I needed time to sort it all out. Just time, that was all—one hour, two? But Rahela didn't understand, at least, not then.

"You despise me like everyone else does," she shouted, rising from her seat. "I knew you would. I was sure you would."

And with that she was off like the wind. I ran after her. I shouted to her. I pled with her to understand—to give her time. I assured her I still loved her. But it was no use. She was gone.

"Let her go," my aunt advised when I returned home. I could hear Rahela upstairs, probably packing her bags.

"But she's got no car," I objected.

"She's got cash. I'll go with her to the railway station. She can get a train or maybe a bus back to Nashville."

"Don't be so hardhearted," I remonstrated petulantly.

"I'm not hardhearted, Mark," Aunt Anna said patiently. "But you both need time. Let her be. She's a strong girl. And she loves you. Point is, do you love her enough to overcome this?"

I put my hand to my head. "I think I do. But Dad? Mom?"

"Pray about it and follow God and your heart," she advised. "It'll work out right in the end."

### 3

I tried to follow my aunt's advice. I prayed for hours. But abortion and Rahela? They didn't seem to go together. If they did, then maybe she wasn't the girl I thought she was.

Dad asked no questions when I returned home for a few days before school restarted. Maybe Aunt Anna had hinted something. Maybe he thought we had broken up and was glad. Maybe....

I had a long talk with Kaye. Rahela had mentioned nothing about the abortion, only the rape. But my twin was not as shocked as I had been. "I am not a bit surprised," she told me. "I wondered if this was Rahela's problem. She seemed so distant at times."

When I returned to Nashville, there was no Rahela. "She's taken one year's leave of absence," I was told by the medical school. "We think she's gone back to Africa."

I found out soon that they were right—she had left without a note, without so much as "Good-bye, it's been nice knowing you." Yet could I blame her when I was the one to blame? I was the coward, or was I? Maybe I was the hero instead—losing my love for the sake of principle. That's what Dad thought when I finally told him. And Mom too. I knew Kaye wasn't so sure about my heroics. "I can't give you advice," she told me. "Follow your heart." As for Aunt Anna, she said nothing. I knew she wasn't pleased with me. And I wasn't pleased with myself. Yet Rahela had expected the impossible. If she had been willing to give me time, to trust me...

The months that followed were the darkest of my whole life. I wrote every week to the Morgan plantation in faraway Kenya but got no response. "Forget about her," my parents advised. But I couldn't. I wouldn't. My roommate seemed to understand, and that was my one comfort. "I'd have reacted the same, Mark," he told me. "But you truly love her and love will win out in the end.

And then one day, I got the longed-for letter.

'I am terribly sorry for running out of your life like I did, Mark," the letter began. "I know I expected too much from you. As you said, I should have given you more time. But, really, it's about far more than the fact I had an abortion. I simply can't fit in the way you can to life in America. And here's why:  Read carefully, Mark. You'll soon see I don't fit into any church; I don't even fit in any political party. I'm simply—unlabeled. Neither you nor anyone else can label me the way you want to, the way you must in order to make me into the kind of clean, honest, conservative, evangelical Christian you have been brought up to be and the kind I deeply admire but know I can't ever be. I'm too confused and, maybe, too honest."

In spite of myself, I soon found my tears nearly almost obliterating the type before me. But I made myself read on.

"I can't be Methodist because I believe in baptism by immersion. It's the Scriptural way as I see it.

"I can't be Baptist because I believe you can lose your salvation."

"I can't be Presbyterian because I can't believe in predestination."

"I can't be Pentecostal because I don't believe that tongues are the evidence of the Holy Spirit's coming to our hearts.

"I can't be Catholic because I can't pray for the dead or believe in purgatory.

"I can't be Eastern Orthodox because I can't worship Mary.

"But that's not the half," she concluded. "I can't be a Republican because I can't agree with them over abortion. If I did, I'd be condemning myself into Hell.

"I can't be a Democrat because I don't agree with them on the Homosexual issue. I believe marriage is between a man and a woman.

"And worse still, Mark," she went on, "I can't fit into your family. I can't be a fundamentalist Christian because of some of the above and because I'm not sure about some things about Genesis, about the world being created in six days, I mean. In fact, I'm not sure about a lot of things. Life has dealt me some hard blows and I'm still stunned.

"So where do you put me? Where *can* you put me? You can't understand what it's like to live in 'the gray zone.' Your God is black and white. My God is gray, Mark. Or He'd better be or He couldn't be my God. But out here in Africa, folks don't always demand clipped, certain answers. We're all too occupied with the business of living. Oh yes, I'm coming back. I need to finish my medical training, need to do something good with my life. The kids dying of aids won't try to label me, will they?

"I had to write this so you have time to think before you meet me again. I still love you, terribly. But I killed my child. Can you live with that? Sometimes I can't. Sometimes I can. And do I really love Christ? Your father doesn't think so and now I sometimes wonder myself. He seems so far away. And yet, when I had that abortion, He was my only comfort. I can't forget that, although I don't feel comforted as I used to. So, when all is said and done, it's far better if you don't come to meet me at the airport. You can't get further involved with someone like myself. So stay away from me, please, or I'll succumb the moment I see you. Try to forget about me. It's best for all of us."

### 4.

By the time Rahela came back as promised, I'd had it out, first with myself and then with Dad. I absolutely knew that Rahela was the girl for me, unlabeled or not. And so I did what she said not to do: I met her at the airport. One look into her face, and she was in my arms. Within two weeks, we were engaged. My parents were furious. Only Aunt Anna and Kaye stood by us. It was hard going, but we were madly in love. I had made up my mind I loved her just as she was—soiled, yes, mixed up, maybe, but still the most wonderful girl I would ever meet. I never took her home, only to Aunt Anna's in Atlanta.

Finally, we both got our degrees. I was a vet; she was a doctor, but it would be several years before she completed all her training and could fulfill her dream. I had agreed to go with her to Kenya. Good vets were needed there in plenty. Meanwhile, we were ready to get married.

It was just a small wedding: Aunt Anna and Rahela's dad, plus some friends who didn't listen to the gossip that Mark Potter was marrying a rank liberal who would take him to hell. Dad couldn't come, he wrote, and keep a clear conscience. Mom followed suite, as usual. But Kaye, bless her heart, was not only there but acted as Rahela's bridesmaid.

And I was happy. I was learning a lot, fast—learning that what mattered most was loving Christ and believing in Him. Maybe I was so happy, I wasn't aware of what was happening to Rahela. Maybe I didn't realize that she had been hurt almost beyond repair. My love and God's love made up for this most of the time. But sometimes it didn't quite.

"I'd give anything to have a label that fits me," she confided one evening as we were sipping our evening drink of hot cocoa.

"But you do," I assured her. "The only label you need is 'a child of God,' isn't it?

Her dark eyes flashed fire and her words had an edge to them I didn't like. "Maybe in some places it is, Mark, but not here, not in good old Christian America!"

"Oh, come on, sweetheart," I remonstrated. "There are plenty of folks who recognize that label and respect and love you as a fellow

Christian. That label is still tied onto you pretty tightly. I see it every day." I leaned over and gave her a kiss and was rewarded with a faint smile. I suppose she was thinking of how we first met.

Then her face darkened again. "You may see it, but your mom and dad don't." Her voice broke.

I took her in my arms as she began to sob almost uncontrollably. "I don't have a mom, Mark," she whispered. "And I could put up with your dad not accepting me, but your mother? It breaks my heart."

"I'm so sorry," I murmured. "So very sorry!"

We sat like that for a few moments, and then she pulled away from me and reached for her handbag. "And there is something else," she muttered. "Something I haven't shared with you."

I frowned. We had promised to share everything, absolutely everything with each other. She saw my frown and said quickly,

"I've only known for a week, Mark, and I just couldn't tell you right away." My heart beat faster. What on earth was she talking about?

I didn't have long to wait. A moment later she had unfolded an airmail letter and was scanning her father's clear, bold handwriting. She held the letter out to me to read, pointing to the last few paragraphs.

"Rahela," I read, "there's something I must tell you for what it's worth. I had a very unexpected letter the other day from someone in Mombasa prison, someone who wronged you beyond words. I never expected to hear from him again and don't know what to make of it. I received it six months ago and hesitated to share it with you, but the prison chaplain has confirmed what the letter said so I feel I must pass on the message in that letter."

I felt the tension in the air as I paused a moment. I glanced at my wife whose face was motionless. "Read on, Mark," was all she said.

I turned back to the letter and read. "The message was this: 'Please tell your daughter how terribly sorry I am for what I did to her. I have come to the Lord while in prison. He has changed my life. I know that for certain. But I have spent weeks of anguish and remorse thinking of how I had ruined several lives, hers, included. I can't expect her to forgive me, but I do want her to know that I am truly, truly sorry. Christ has forgiven me and that is a comfort. And I pray every day for Rahela that He might heal the hurt I caused, and that she might lead a happy and fulfilled life in spite of all I did to her."

I looked up at my wife as I folded the letter and gave it back to her. I was about to say, "Well, that's good news isn't it?" and then it hit me! This profession of faith by a rapist, if genuine, turned everything upside down. No wonder Rahela had seemed so conflicted the last few days.

"So, Mark," she asked, looking straight into my eyes, "What do I do now? Forgive? Forget? Live happily ever after knowing if monsters can be transformed, just like that, then I certainly should have not aborted my baby?"

Her words faded away. I was stunned by what she had just said. But she hadn't finished. "And more than that," she went on slowly, "I am obliged to forgive him. I should have done so a long time ago but I haven't. And the fact that he may be changed should make it easier, but it doesn't."

She threw down the letter and stood to her feet. Her dark eyes flashed fire. "Anyway, I really don't believe a word of it."

To tell the truth, I didn't either, not really. And yet…..?

"Maybe we should go and see for ourselves, Rahela." The words were out before I could stop them. She gave me a horrified look and then shook her head.

"Impossible, Mark!" she muttered. "You can't expect me to do that, can you?"

"No," I agreed, taking her hand and squeezing it. "No, I can't. Although I could go."

She shook her head again. "Maybe someday," she murmured, "but not now. We're newly married and I'm determined not to let anything spoil our lives. Let's wait a while. I'll ask Dad to keep a check on..." She hesitated. "On *him!* If he's phony, then it'll soon show once his prison term is up."

I nodded. "You're right as usual, darling." I drew her close. "Time sorts out many things if we'll let it. And it does something else, too!"

"What's that?" she murmured.

"Makes you grow more beautiful every day and more beloved."

A smile curved her lips. "Ditto," she whispered.

"Ditto? I'm flattered!"

"I meant 'ditto' to the last part of your statement. As for the first...."

I silenced her with a kiss. I could feel her body relaxing in my arms. And I wondered, as we went to sleep that night, what I had done to deserve such bliss!

# Chapter Five
## Not again, Mark!
### 1.

It was our second wedding anniversary. I loved my wife more than ever. We still were estranged from my parents, but that didn't stop us being happy together.

And of course, I prayed for a child. And at last, Rahela got pregnant. She was over the moon. All went well until her fourth month. She came back from her weekly checkup puzzled.

"He wants to see us both next week. Something's wrong Mark. I can feel it in my bones," she warned.

I tried to laugh away her fears, but my heart was beating wildly as we walked into the doctor's office that Monday morning.

"Sit down," the doctor said kindly.

We sat facing him. I grabbed Rahela's hand and held it tightly.

I'll come to the point immediately," Dr. Rathbone told us. "Mr. Potter, your wife's condition is such that if she has this baby, it could kill her. I recommend an abortion, immediately."

I felt Rahela's hand go limp in mine. Then there was a thud and she had slipped to the floor. It took some time to bring her round but at last, the color drained back into her face.

"I know it's a shock," the doctor said compassionately. "But it's the only safe thing to do. Go home and talk it over, only if it is to be done, it must be done very soon."

That night I rocked my distraught wife in my arms for hours as I hoped I would soon rock the baby that we both wanted so badly.

"Not again, Mark!" she wailed. "I just can't do it the second time." I tried to reason with her, but she was adamant and as the hours passed she became more so. "I won't do it, Mark," she said. "I'd rather die."

"But this is different," I assured her. "No one will condemn you for this, at least not anyone I know."

"But what about me, Mark?" she asked piteously. "One abortion in a lifetime, whatever the reason, is more than most women can cope with. But two? Don't ask it of me, please."

I held her very tight and prayed. Anything more was beyond my power to do. Finally, we told our families about our dilemma. And it was then that something strange happened. "Your wife's life comes first," Dad told me. I looked at him in shock.

"But she refuses, Dad," I sobbed. "She can't go through it all again."

Dad understood in the end, and so did Mom and Kaye and Aunt Anna and so did my father-in-law. But inwardly, I couldn't accept Rahela's decision. But then, I'd never had an abortion before.

"Maybe the doctor's fears are groundless," Mom told me.

"Maybe," I agreed.

One night, when we couldn't sleep and began to talk the night away as we often did, Rahela told me she had gone again to the doctor and asked him something. I could feel her body tense as she talked.

"I told him about my abortion, Mark," she confessed, "and asked if he thought giving birth to the child would have endangered my life back then."

There was a long pause and then she collapsed in tears in my arms. I held her tight. "The irony is, Mark, that I couldn't have given birth safely anyway."

I was speechless. "But you would have had to carry it for nine months," I whispered.

She nodded. "Yes, and that's what I couldn't face. But this child," and she patted her abdomen as she spoke, "this child is yours and mine, Mark. It is blessed. And..." her voice broke, "even if I don't make it through the delivery, I'll carry it praying, and weeping, and praising."

And then she began to sing. I always loved her singing, but that night it was as if the angels had invaded our bedroom. "Great is thy faithfulness," she sang, "Lord unto me."

## 2.

Days passed into weeks, the weeks into months, and her due date grew nearer. Mom and Dad were constant visitors in our home and it wasn't long before they were almost as much in love with, my wife as I was.

Rahela was in the seventh heaven, in spite of her very uncertain future. "I have a mom again," she would tell me almost every day. "And what a mom!"

"Yes, she is something else," I admitted.

"I've told her nearly everything, Mark," Rahela confessed. "And last night, when you and your dad were out and we were alone, she prayed with me and I forgave Douglas."

I stared at my wife in shock. I couldn't believe my ears. Firstly, she had forgiven the man who had almost ruined her life and secondly, she had called him by his name, something she had never ever done as far as I knew.

"That's wonderful," I told her when I could find my tongue again. I used the word 'wonderful' almost automatically, but when I thought about it for a moment I realized that this announcement of Rahela's, if I were absolutely honest, troubled me.

Rahela could read me like a book. "What's wrong, Mark?" she asked placing her hand on my shoulder.

"I…..I…" I stammered. She waited patiently while I tried to formulate my feelings. "I think it is wonderful for you, Rahela, but I'm not sure I can forgive him, especially if….if…."

I laid my head on her shoulder and wept, something I very rarely did. "Give it time, Mark," she whispered. "I know you and you will forgive Douglas…in time."

The name, somehow, jarred on me. Rahela had never ever given the guy a name before. "Douglas?" I repeated. "That's not a Kenyan name, is it? Isn't it unusual for native Kenyans to give their children such a very English name?"

Rahela looked stunned. Her face held an odd expression. "So you thought he was an African?" she asked, smiling faintly.

"Yes, of course."

"Why, 'of course,' Mark?" she wanted to know.

There was a long silence as my wife waited patiently for my answer. "Because," I admitted slowly, "I assumed that a worker on your plantation would be a native Kenyan."

Rahela gave a long sigh. "Be honest, Mark," she urged.

"Honest?" I repeated. "What on earth makes you think I'm not honest?"

"Because I had this very same conversation with your Mom the other day."

"And?"

Rahela sighed again. This was obviously very difficult for her. "And…" she began slowly, "she admitted that it had seemed obvious to her that someone who had committed such a crime would be an African not a 'civilized' white."

I got up from my chair and began to pace the floor. I had thought myself Rahela's savior of sorts—her knight in shining armor. But it was she, the condemned one, the 'soiled' one, who forgave more quickly and who seemed as free of prejudice as the Almighty himself.

"Let's pray," I told her, dropping on my knees. "And you pray first," I begged. "I think you have a line to Heaven these days!"

Rahela knelt beside me and began to pray and oh, how she prayed…. for me…for herself….for our baby…..for Douglas…..

and for the whole fallen world around us. And then, when she had finished she nudged me gently.

"It's your turn, Mark," she reminded me.

Yes, it was certainly my turn, but all I could manage through my tears was "Dear God, I'm dreadfully sorry. Please, please forgive me!"

And He did forgive me, then and there. And Heaven seemed to fill our little living-room.

"Mark," Rahela told me as we sipped our evening cocoa, "I don't feel unlabeled anymore. I am out of the gray zone at last and into the clear light of His love. He has labeled me His child. What more do I want or need? Sometimes He is so bright, so clear, I can't stand looking at His love. But if we don't trust God in the gray zone, we won't recognize Him in the Light, will we?"

For an answer, I hugged her tighter and thought, "Yes, wifie, you're miles ahead of me here. But wait for me, for I'm coming too!"

### 3.

I'd like to say that everything went well, that our prayers were answered, that Rahela made it through the birthing process safely. But that's not what happened. I did lose my wonderful wife that sunny July day, the same day that our tiny daughter was born. And Rahela was buried in our family plot, with the simple inscription written on the headstone, "Rahela Gabriella Potter—'a child of God.'"

I often go to her grave, sometimes alone, sometimes with little Rahela, Mom, Dad, and Kaye. We go there not just because we can never forget my brave, wonderful wife, but because we all know that she influenced all our lives. Our friends often don't understand why Dad has changed so much, but I do.

Life goes on much the same. I'm a vet, but preach part time. I've never married again. I don't need to or want to. Mom babysits every day. Great Aunt Anna has long since passed away.

And my father-in-law? He visits us every year and dotes on his little granddaughter who is growing more like her mother every day. We often visit my wife's grave together and share precious memories. But, apart from me, it's my dad who goes there most often.

"It took her death to change me," he confided one evening six months after we had buried the best woman on earth.

"How, Dad?" I wanted to know.

"I've given up trying to label people, Mark," he said with a half-smile. "Well that's not true. I still label them only…"

"Only there's only one label that matters, right?"

"Right, Son, right." He put his arm on my shoulder. "A child of God?"

"Yes, Dad. "A child of God."

# Epilogue
## Back to Africa
### 1.

Mark Potter fingered the manila envelope with reverence. He looked down fondly at his wife's grave and then back at the envelope. His father had just handed him this letter written by Rahela just before her death.

"I was to give it to you after five years, Mark," his dad had told him. "But only on two conditions."

"Conditions?" Mark repeated, frowning a little. "What were they?"

"You'll soon find out when you read the letter," was all the answer he received. "But obviously they've been fulfilled, otherwise I wouldn't be giving it to you, would I?"

His father gave an enigmatic smile and strode off leaving Mark with mixed emotions. Of course he was thrilled to hold this "surprise" letter in his hands. Anything written by his beloved Rahela would be prized and cherished. But "conditions?" He wasn't sure he liked that word.

Mark took the letter and sat down under the shade of a nearby tree. Tremblingly, he tore open the envelope and took out a piece of folded notepaper. His heart beat faster. It was as if Rahela stood beside him, watching as he began to read.

"My very dearest husband," the letter began. "I feel I must write this letter before I leave you. I love you so very much. You took me to your heart when others rejected me. You were even willing to be an outcast in your own family in order to be my husband. So is it any wonder I want the very best for you? So, dearest Mark, remember that I probably know you better than you do yourself. So read on, trusting a woman's foresight and God's providence! They've done a lot for you, admit it. So don't fight them now.

"I gave this letter to your father before I went into labor. I told him to give it to you in five years' time on two conditions: 1. That you had never remarried. 2. That Amanda Perkins remained single also."

"Amanda Perkins!" Mark repeated to himself, wrinkling his brow. "Now what does Amanda have to do with my life? I'm doing fine and so is our daughter. Well, maybe I'm jumping the gun. I'd better read on before making any conclusions."

"Amanda loves you, Mark," he read. "She has always loved you. And if I had not come on the scene, you two might well be married by now. Now, don't crumple up the letter at this point but read on, please!"

Mark smiled in spite of his frustration. Rahela could read him like a book. "Your loyalty to me will keep you from reality, Mark. Honestly it will! But your mother can't take care of our child forever. So listen to me: If you think you could never love Amanda as you should love a wife, then disregard everything I've written up till now. But if..... I don't think I need to finish the sentence.

"I know you shouldn't need my permission to remarry but being Mark Potter of impeccable loyalty and principle, you probably do. So you have it. And not only my permission, but my blessing."

Mark put down the letter and wept. He wept as he never wept since he buried Rahela. And then he laughed. How he laughed! And then he prayed for perhaps an hour, under that oak tree. He was about to make his way back to the house when he realized he had not finished the letter.

"One thing more," Rahela had written. "I'm not sure if you ever told Douglas, the man who wronged me those years ago, that you forgave him also. If you haven't, then, please do it now. More than that, I'd like you to visit my old home at least once, and, if possible take our daughter with you. Show her my mother's grave and my old haunts, please, if you possibly can.

"Now, put my letter away, and do what your heart directs you. I know you will never forget me and that we will meet once more in a place where everyone wears the same label—'A forgiven child of God!'

"Love you forever and forever,

"Your own Rahela."

## 2.

Mark's heart beat wildly as he knocked on Pastor Jim's office door. In a few moments he would meet the man who had haunted his dreams for years. Yes, he had said he had forgiven him those years ago and felt God's peace flood his heart. But that was in the safety of a cozy little living room in the hills of Tennessee, thousands of miles away. Now he was coming face to face with the man he had called a "villain" for years. And while the knowledge that he was white, not black as he had long supposed, had shocked him at first, it had not made things easier.

"Douglas will be here in a moment," the pastor was saying, and his voice sounded miles away. "It might help you to know that he is terribly nervous about meeting you, even though he has been told that you forgive him."

Mark's lips twitched slightly. "If he only knew how nervous I am too! But, pastor, I don't feel terribly forgiving right now. And I'm afraid…"

Pastor Jim laid a hand on Mark's arm. "I'd be the same if I were in your place," he assured him kindly. "We are all human, Mark, although forgiven. And it's not your feelings that matter right now."

"No?"

"No, surprising as that may sound. It's your actions. You have come thousands of miles to see this man and assure him you forgive him. Now, trust the spirit of our forgiving Christ to speak through you when you meet him. Will you do that?"

Mark nodded then looked up as the door opened behind him and a very tall and very large middle-aged man entered the small office. He seemed to fill the room with his presence. Mark felt like a dwarf beside him. Tattoos covered every available part of his body. "Typical thug," was Mark's first impression.

"Douglas, this is Mark Potter," Pastor Jim began. Douglas took a step towards Mark then hesitated. This was worse than he thought. This giant of a man had taken advantage of not only Rahela but of other women also. He was, in plain terms, a "rapist." He had stolen something so precious from his beloved, made her feel unclean, unwanted, and…..unlabeled.

But then, something told him, probably the Holy Spirit, to look into the man's eyes. Mark forced himself to do so. They were deep blue eyes, troubled eyes, fearful eyes, but penetrating eyes that pierced Mark's soul. He remembered the pastor's words and knew what he had to do.

Mark said later his hand had never felt as leaden as it did at that moment. But lead or no lead, he made it extend towards the man he had come so far to meet. And as he did so, all changed.

"I forgive you, Douglas," Mark said. "And so did Rahela."

The man's grip tightened. Mark heard one, long, deep sob coming from somewhere very deep inside and then they were embracing. Tears were flowing everywhere.

Pastor Jim began to sing: "Amazing Grace," in his deep baritone voice and soon Mark and even Douglas had joined in. And it seemed that Mark heard another voice, a pure silver-toned soprano, join in the melody.

There is no need to relate what followed. Joy, celebration, and honesty on all sides. Douglas was not completely out of the woods yet. He was on probation and struggled a lot with his past. But the direction he was headed was upward, Pastor Jim told Mark later. And with Mark's forgiveness deep in his heart, Douglas would make even quicker strides towards complete freedom.

His father-in-law was waiting for him as he exited the church office. Little Rahela ran to meet her father.

"Is Douglas coming home with us?" she wanted to know.

"Not now," Mark said smiling. "But some day we will all be Home together with your mother and everyone who loves the Lord Jesus."

"But now," the little girl said decidedly, "now we're going to our Tennessee home, aren't we Grandpa?"

Grandpa Morgan nodded. "Yes. We have to go home. The wedding is set for a week today. Remember?"

Rahela clapped her hands together in glee. "Yes. And Amanda says I'm to be the flower girl. I'm so sorry Mummy can't be there. But then, if she was there, Amanda wouldn't be marrying you, would she, Daddy?"

There was an awkward silence and then Mark said softly. "You're right. But your mummy will be there in spirit, Rahela. Remember that."

The child nodded. "Yes, Daddy. I can't ever forget. Mummy has only been with me in spirit ever since I was born."

Tears filled Mark's eyes. As always his little daughter got to the heart of the matter.

"Don't cry, Daddy," Rahela said throwing herself into his arms. "Marrying Amanda makes things ever so much better. But what about Douglas? I want to see him, Daddy. I like seeing people who knew Mummy when she was young."

Mark and his father-in-law exchanged glances. Glen Morgan gave a slight nod and smile. Mark held Rahela tightly in his arms as he whispered. "I'll tell you a secret, sweetheart. In a few months, you, Amanda, Grandpa Potter, and I will be coming here to Kenya to live and we'll see Douglas and all Mummy's old friends all the time. How will you like that?"

Rahela thought a moment. "I'll like it fine now that Grandma Potter's gone to heaven. So we'll all be family together and that's what matters. But what will you do here, Daddy?"

Mark held her tight. "Well, with the two Grandpas' help, we're going to build a home for unwanted children, sweetheart."

"That's what Mummy wanted to do, isn't it?" the child asked, stroking Mark's face.

"Yes. It's exactly what she wanted."

"Then she must be singing in Heaven, she's so happy. Right?"

"Right!" Mark agreed, smiling.

"And what'll we call this Home, Daddy?"

Mark thought a moment. "I'm not sure, Rahela. But whatever we call it, we'll put somewhere the words: "In memory of Rahela Morgan Potter.""

"We could call it "Rahela's children," the little girl suggested. "How about that?"

"Why not!" Mark exclaimed. "Or something like it. I think Mummy would like that.....very much!"